SING SOME MORE!

Written by **Deborah Diesen** • Illustrated by **Howard Gray**

We're the birds that make the music
That you hear up in the trees,

And we vocalize with gusto
As we hit the notes with ease.

With our chirps and our arpeggios,
We sing just what we please!

And when we're DONE?

We
sing
some
MORE!

We begin our day ahead of dawn
Before a hint of light.

As the sun begins to show itself
We sing with all our might.

First we solo from our perches,

Then we sing as we take flight.

And when we're DONE?

We sing some MORE!

We perform our songs for others
And we hope they'll sing along.

We have tunes for all occasions,
And our harmonies are strong.

We create new music daily,

And it never comes out wrong.

And when we're DONE?

We sing some!

MORE!

Oh, our voices each are lovely,
But together they are grand!

With our a cappella talents
We do not require a band.

We sing ballads! We do anthems!

We're a vocal wonderland!

And when we're DONE?

We sing some

We have endless dedication
To our craft and to our art,

And throughout the day, we give our all
To each and every part.

Yes, we throw ourselves into our work!

We sing straight from the heart!

And when we're DONE?

WE SING SOME

The slowly setting sun
Does not discourage us a bit,

For we know our birdy melodies

Are sure to be a hit.

Yes, we sing
       and sing

and sing
          and sing

And we will never quit!

And when we're DONE?

Well, actually...

"I think we're really done."

"Yeah, I'm pretty tired."

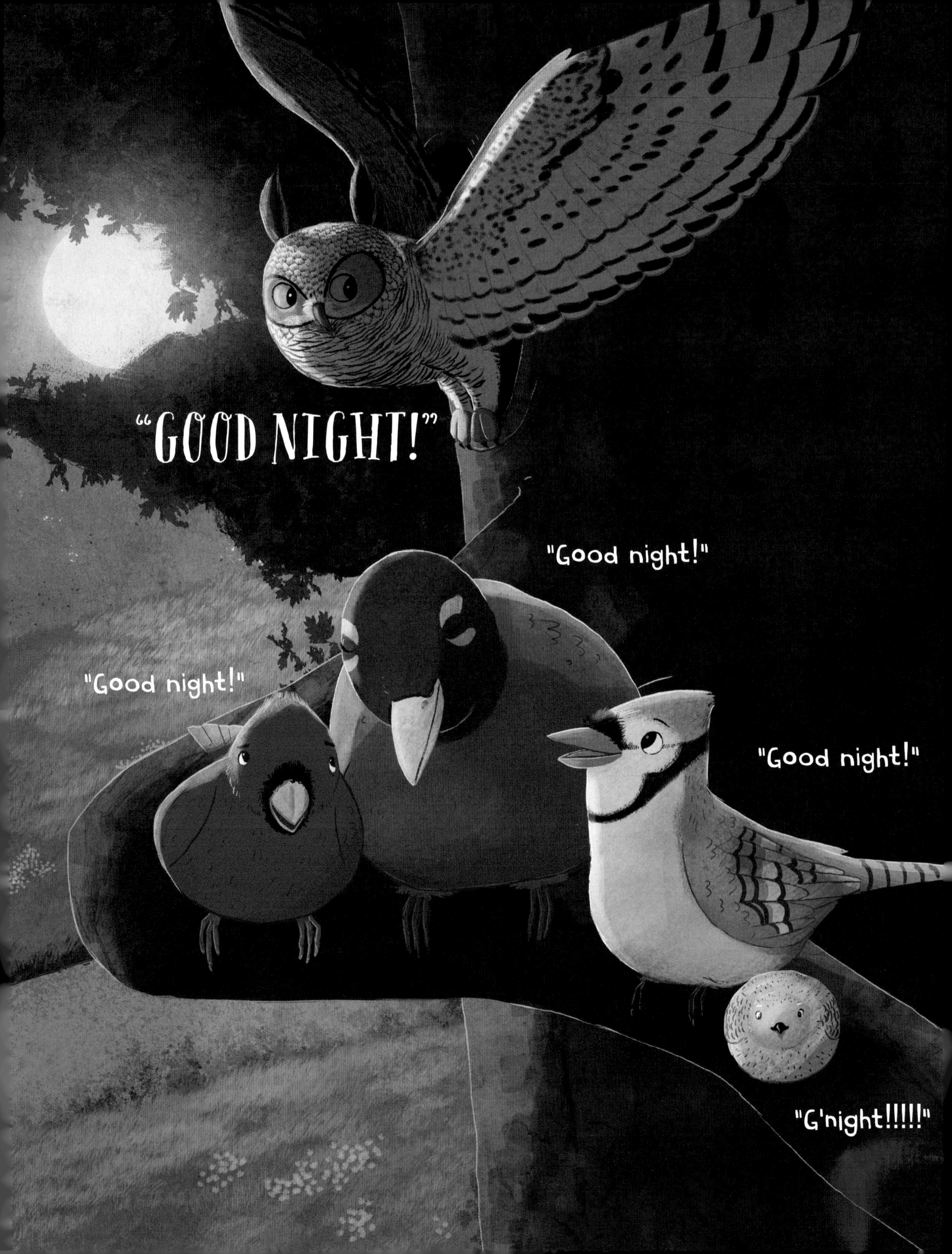
"GOOD NIGHT!"
"Good night!"
"Good night!"
"Good night!"
"G'night!!!!!"

But TOMORROW...

WE'LL
SING
SOME

MOOOOO

OOOORE!

A cappella: singing without instruments

Anthems: songs of praise or patriotism

Arpeggios: notes of a chord sung or played one right after the other

Ballads: slow songs

Harmonies: combinations of musical notes or pitches

Gusto: enthusiastic enjoyment

Melodies: rhythmic tunes made from notes sung or played together

Solo: a piece of music performed by a single voice

Vocalize: to give voice to or sing

For Abby, who loves bird-watching.
—*Debbie*

♪

For Mum!
—*Howard*

SLEEPING BEAR PRESS™

2395 South Huron Parkway, Suite 200 | Ann Arbor, MI 48104 | www.sleepingbearpress.com

Printed and bound in the United States.

10 9 8 7 6 5 4 3 2 1

Library of Congress Cataloging-in-Publication Data: Names: Diesen, Deborah, author. | Gray, Howard (Howard Willem Ian), illustrator. Title: Sing some more / written by Deborah Diesen; illustrated by Howard Gray. Description: Ann Arbor, Michigan : Sleeping Bear Press, [2020] | Audience: Ages 4-8. | Summary: From before sunrise until after sunset, a group of birds sings and sings some more, first performing solos from their perches and then harmonizing while in flight. | Identifiers: LCCN 2020007409 | ISBN 9781534110526 (hardcover) Subjects: CYAC: Birds–Fiction. | Birdsongs–Fiction. | Classification: LCC PZ7.D57342 Sin 2020 | DDC [E]–dc23 LC record available at https://lccn.loc.gov/2020007409